Mrs Dippy and her Amazing Inventions

Written by Tony Mitton

Illustrated by An

Contents

Mrs Dippy's Dog

Mrs Dippy was in her workshop. There was a knock on the door. It was PC Best, the local policeman.

'Hello, Mrs Dippy,' he said. 'I've come to warn you. There's a gang of thieves about, so keep your doors and windows locked. And don't leave anything lying around. Have you got a burglar alarm?'

'Not yet,' said Mrs Dippy. 'But I soon will have. Leave it to me.'

Mrs Dippy went to her storeroom to look for useful bits.

Her storeroom was full of old machines that had broken down and were no use to anyone else any more. But Mrs Dippy was a clever woman. She could make amazing things with bits and bobs. Before long she had got together an interesting little pile of this and that. She put the bits in a cart and pulled the cart into her workshop.

Mrs Dippy laid out the bits neatly on the floor. She looked at them thoughtfully. There was an old dustbin without a lid. There were lots of empty tin cans. There were bits of old hoover tube, pieces of pipe, electric wire from lamps and broken bicycle lights. There were even parts from radios.

It looked a mess and a muddle. But slowly, carefully, Mrs Dippy began to put them together. As she worked she talked quietly to herself.

By the next day her work was nearly done. Mrs Dippy stood back and gave it a long, hard look. Yes, not bad. It did look just about right. And what did it look like? Why, a dog of course!

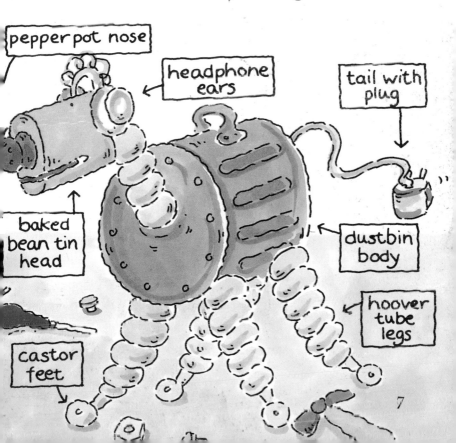

pepper pot nose

headphone ears

tail with plug

baked bean tin head

dustbin body

hoover tube legs

castor feet

It had a dustbin body, four legs on castors, a doggy head with a pepper pot for a nose and a not-very-waggly tail. That was because there was a plug on the end of it. The plug was for charging up its battery. For this was no ordinary dog – it was a robot dog.

Mrs Dippy liked the look of her electric dog. He seemed like a very good robot dog indeed. 'But you do look a bit dented, don't you?' she murmured. 'Of course. That's what I'll call you. I name this dog, Dent,' she said, cracking open a can of *Diet Pupsi*. 'You'll be better than an alarm, won't you?' she said. 'You'll keep those thieves away! But first I'll need to turn you into a real guard dog. To begin with, you'll need a loud bark.'

Mrs Dippy opened a little door in Dent's head. There were wires inside.

She got to work with the wires and soon it was done.

'Let's hear it,' said Mrs Dippy, standing back.

'Buzz wuzz!' barked Dent.

'That will have to do for now,'
said Mrs Dippy. 'Let's see to your
eyes next.'

She put some bits of a bike light on
Dent's eyes to make him look fierce.
'If you see a thief these fierce eyes
will flash red, on and off,' she told
him. 'Now I need to tighten your
nuts and bolts a bit, so keep still for
a moment.' Mrs Dippy took out her
big spanner from her pocket.

When Dent saw the spanner his eyes lit up. He thought the spanner was a big, metal bone. So he grabbed it in his mouth and ran off into the garden.

'Come back here at once,' shouted Mrs Dippy.

But Dent was too busy with the spanner to hear her. He was digging a hole to bury it in.

Mrs Dippy led Dent back inside. 'I think you need a bit more fixing,' she said crossly.

She looked at Dent's wires and did some more work. Then she stood back.

'There!' she said proudly. But Dent wagged his head instead of his tail. Then he began to walk backwards.

'Hmmm,' said Mrs Dippy, 'you need more practice. Come on. Time for walkies.'

Mrs Dippy and Dent set out for the park. On the way, Dent kept turning round in circles. Every time he passed a lamp post he tried to bite it. Mrs Dippy frowned as she pulled him along.

When they got to the park Mrs Dippy let him off the lead. Dent ran straight to the pond. He jumped in with a splash and began to chase the model boats.

'Buzz wuzz, buzz wuzz!' he barked with great excitement. He thought they were robot ducks.

Buzz
Wuzz

'Come away, you silly dog. Come and fetch some sticks,' called Mrs Dippy.

She began to throw sticks all over the place.

'Go and fetch, boy! Fetch, Dent!' she shouted.

Dent ran off. When he came back his mouth was full of umbrellas. A lot of angry people were chasing him.

Just then a motor mower went by.
It was mowing the grass by the pond.
Dent stopped. He dropped the
umbrellas and growled. He thought
the mower was another robot dog
like him.

'Grrrr,' he growled.

'Brrrr,' the motor mower seemed
to say back.

Dent ran at it with his red eyes
flashing on and off. BANG! He
crashed into it and picces went flying
everywhere.

It took Mrs Dippy and the gardener a long time to sort out all the pieces. But in the end they had two neat piles – one for Dent, the other for the mower. Mrs Dippy borrowed the gardener's wheelbarrow to take Dent's bits back home. When she got there she took out her plans and got down to work.

'This time I'll be much more careful,' she said. 'Here goes.'

Mrs Dippy got very busy in her workshop.

'I think this goes here,' she said, 'and I think this goes here, too. But I'm not sure where this goes… Hmmm. Let me see now…'

She was so busy that she did not notice the thief creeping into her garden. He was just about to steal some of her best apples from her prize apple tree.

'There!' said Mrs Dippy, sounding pleased with herself. 'I think that's right. Let's try you out in the garden. Come on, Dent!'

She opened the door and Dent ran out at once, almost knocking her over. His eyes were flashing. The thief took one look at him and jumped straight up into a tree. He clung up in the branches for dear life. But Dent had not seen the thief – nor had Mrs Dippy.

For Dent was running up and down the garden nibbling away furiously at the grass. He seemed to think he was a lawnmower!

The thief crawled along the branch and quickly jumped over the garden wall.

'It's time to move on, mates,' said the terrified thief to his gang.

'There's an iron dog on our trail.
It's got red eyes and terrible teeth.
It runs around growling and chewing
up everything in its way. It nearly
chewed me up too. I'm not staying
around here to be crunched up by a
mad, metal dog.'

'Yeah,' said the boss, 'let's get out
of here.'

'Back to work again I think, Dent,' said Mrs Dippy. 'You seem to have some bits of mower mixed up inside you. Never mind. We'll get you right in the end.' And she started to hum again as she peered at her plans.

Just at that moment, PC Best poked his head through her window. 'It seems those thieves have gone,' he said. 'We found their hideout empty and they were seen driving away very fast indeed.'

'That's nice,' said Mrs Dippy. 'Now where does this wire go…?'

What happened when Dent saw the motor mower?

How did Dent stop the thief?

Mrs Dippy's Helper

Mrs Dippy was at the kitchen sink.
She was up to her elbows in soap
suds and washing-up. She had been
so busy inventing, that there were
two days' worth of dishes to do. Just
at that moment a cat appeared at the
kitchen window.

Dent the robot dog sat up
suddenly. 'Buzz wuzz!' he growled as
his eyes flashed red. He turned
round in quick circles, madly
knocking his oil can over. The oil
went all over the kitchen floor.

'More work!' said Mrs Dippy, crossly wiping the suds from her hands.

'It's no good,' muttered Mrs Dippy. 'I can't be an inventor and do the housework. I need a helper.'

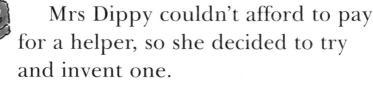

Mrs Dippy couldn't afford to pay for a helper, so she decided to try and invent one.

'Let's see what's in the storeroom at the moment,' she said to herself.

In the storeroom was a whole heap of junk with an old telephone on top. 'That will be good for speaking orders into,' thought Mrs Dippy. 'I can't wait to begin.'

So she took a pile of bits to her workshop and started to invent her robot. It was going to do all the things she didn't like doing. As she sat drawing the plans, Dent could hear her murmuring to herself.

'Rubber gloves so the washing-up doesn't rust his hands. Two old wellingtons so he can mop the floors without foot rust. A feather duster to come out on a metal rod. Ah! A dust-sniffer to make it work. Mmm…yes…'

When she had finished planning, she took out her tools and started to build her robot. For quite a long while, she hammered and banged and welded and fiddled and screwed. The robot began to grow. It was soon time to get to work on the brain.

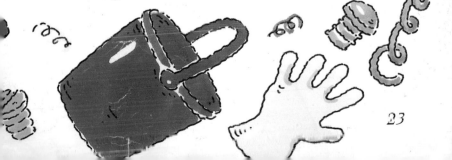

But while Mrs Dippy was fiddling
around inside the brainbox, Dent saw
her spanner. He thought it was a big
metal bone and he grabbed it in his
mouth and ran off into the garden
with it. Mrs Dippy rushed after him.

Mrs Dippy chased Dent around the
garden, trying to get her spanner back.

She had left the kitchen door
open and the little cat at the window
slipped in quietly. When it saw the
coloured wires inside the robot's
brainbox, it went crazy. This was
much better than a ball of wool!

By the time Mrs Dippy came back
in with her spanner the wires were in
a complete tangle. 'What a mess!'
cried Mrs Dippy as she shooed the
little cat away.

'Now how were these wires meant
to go?' said Mrs Dippy to herself.
'Was it green to red and blue to
brown and the plain ones together?
Or was it... Let me see now,' she
tutted as she fiddled and fixed.

Dent sat very quietly while Mrs Dippy worked. She had taken out his battery as a punishment. 'That'll keep him quiet while I do this important fiddly bit,' she said firmly.

After quite a lot of fiddling and fixing the robot was finished. It looked like a robot that was going to be really useful around the house. Mrs Dippy stood back and beamed at it with pride.

'Mrs Dippy's little helper,' she almost sang with joy, though actually the robot was rather tall. 'As you're going to do so much housework, I think I'll call you "Drudge". That's a nice name for a robot, isn't it, Dent?' But Dent did not reply. Mrs Dippy had still not put his battery back in.

'I can't wait to try you out,' said Mrs Dippy, tightening Drudge's last few screws.

Mrs Dippy gave Drudge his first ever jobs. 'Right, Drudge. Do you hear me loud and clear? I want you to do four things:

Do the dishes. Wash and hang out my dirty socks. Hoover the carpet Mow the lawn.

'Oh…and bring me a pot of tea,' she added. 'I'm going to watch telly. The *Runaway Robots* is on in a few minutes. That's a film I've always wanted to see. Come on, Dent, bring my slippers and come and lie down by the telly with me. I can use you to rest my feet on. No! Those are my wellies, silly dog. I asked for my slippers. What's the matter with your ears?'

Just as the film was getting interesting there was a *bleep bleep bleep* sound and Drudge came rattling in with a tray of tea. It looked perfect. The teapot had a cosy on it, the cup and saucer were clean, the milk was in a little jug and the sugar was in a small bowl with a shiny spoon. There was even a fresh dish of oil for Dent.

'Bliss,' murmured Mrs Dippy. 'This is the life!'

When the adverts came on Mrs Dippy gave Dent his dish of oil. As he lapped it up, she poured herself a cup of tea. She lifted it to her lips with a smile.

'Yuck!' spat Mrs Dippy. 'What's this?' The tea tasted terrible. She fished around in the teapot with the teaspoon. Something soggy and smelly and wet came out of it. It was one of her socks. 'Oh no…!' she sighed, 'Whatever has that robot done?' And she went to find out.

Her fluffy carpet in the front room looked very strange. It seemed to have gone bald. And there in the corner was the lawn mower. Its box for cuttings was full of dusty wool.

'Oh, no!' shrieked Mrs Dippy. 'He's mown the carpet. My best fluffy carpet is ruined. It will never grow back unless I invent something really clever. I should have been more careful after the cat got into his wires. I wonder what else he's gone and done,' and she went out to look in the garden.

The garden was actually looking very tidy. The grass hadn't been mown, but it did look very neat and clean.

'This looks all right,' said Mrs Dippy, looking at the lawn. 'I wonder what he's done here?'

Then she saw the hoover. It was standing on the edge of the lawn. 'I see,' she began to say. 'Mow the carpet, hoover the lawn. That's back to front, isn't it? And the tea was made with my dirty sock. So that means... yes, I thought so,' she sighed as she looked across to the washing line.

Everything on the line was beautifully arranged. Drudge had hung it out so carefully and neatly. The things all dangled there, sparkling cleanly in the sunshine. But there were no socks, and no other kind of laundry either – just cups and saucers and plates and knives and forks.

'I thought so,' said Mrs Dippy. 'He's hung the washing-up on the washing line. Ah well...!'

'I'm glad I decided to video that film,' said Mrs Dippy. She was out in the garden with the laundry basket, unpegging the dry dishes to take back into the kitchen. After that she had to empty the twigs and leaves out of the hoover bag and put the hoover back indoors. Then she had to throw the carpet cuttings away and think of an invention for re-growing carpets. And then there were her socks that needed saving from the teapot.

'Little helper, indeed!' she muttered crossly.

BUZZ WUZZ

While Mrs Dippy was busy working Drudge had settled down in front of the telly.

'I say,' he bleeped. 'Isn't this sofa comfy? Ooh, I like the look of this film. Just my kind of thing. I wonder what this sock tea tastes like? Mmm, not bad – sort of cheesy. I think I'll have a bit more. Well, this beats being in bits in a dusty old storeroom, eh Dent?'

'Buzz wuzz,' Dent agreed, looking out at a very busy Mrs Dippy.

What were all the things that Drudge did wrong?

Mrs Dippy's Car

It was an ordinary morning at Mrs Dippy's. Dent the robot dog was plugged in to get his battery working. Drudge the robot was busy watching telly. And Mrs Dippy was at the breakfast table reading the paper.

'It says there's going to be lots of sunny weather,' said Mrs Dippy.

'I think we need a rest from the housework,' she carried on, looking hard at Drudge. 'Let's have a day out.' The two robots sat up suddenly.

'We could go walking in the mountains,' said Mrs Dippy.

'That would be too tiring,' bleeped Drudge.

'Well, what about visiting the big city?' tried Mrs Dippy.

'Crackle, crackle – too noisy – too many machines,' buzzed Dent.

'I know!' cried Mrs Dippy. 'How about the seaside? Lots of sand to dig in for Dent. And Drudge can just lie down on it and rest.'

'Perfect!' crackled the two robots together.

'Hmm. How are we going to get there?' muttered Mrs Dippy. She was surrounded by maps and timetables and Drudge was looking over her shoulder. 'There are no trains or buses to the best beaches. And it's much too far to walk.' Drudge nodded. He didn't want to walk. 'We need a car, really. Most people go by car. But I can't afford one.'

Dent started scratching at the door to the storeroom.

'Of course!' said Mrs Dippy. 'Clever dog. I can invent one, can't I?'

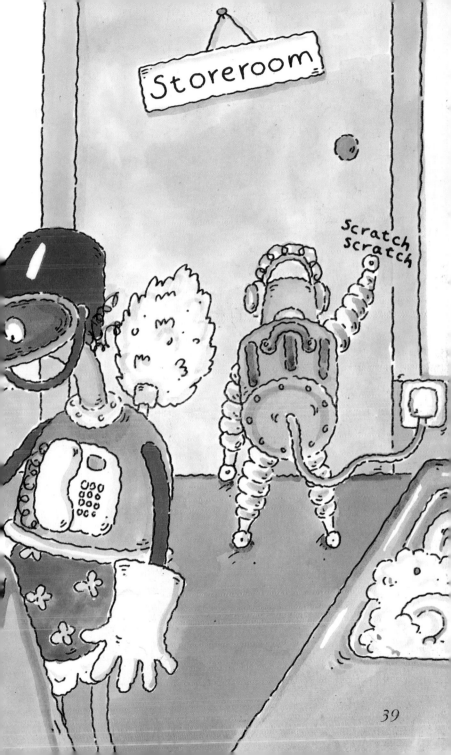

The storeroom was nearly empty. So Mrs Dippy took her hand-cart and went to the junk yard. Drudge and Dent climbed in and went along for the ride.

'How much for them?' asked the junk man, pointing to the two robots.

'They're not for sale,' said Mrs Dippy crossly. 'We've come to buy bits for a car.'

Drudge and Dent liked the junk yard. It felt cosy to them. They helped Mrs Dippy to make a pile of useful-looking bits.

Some of the things they piled up
to make the car with were: an old sofa,
pram wheels, umbrellas for a roof,
and a washing machine for the engine
(good for making a clean getaway!)

'Did you say these were for making
a car?' asked the junk man, scratching
his head and looking puzzled.

'Well, more of a beach-buggy,
really,' said Mrs Dippy. 'We'll take
this whole pile here, thank you.'

When they got home, the two robots helped Mrs Dippy spread the bits out on the floor of her workshop. They wanted to watch her make the car. While Mrs Dippy worked they kept interrupting her.

'Will it talk like us?' asked Dent.

'Will it do the hoovering instead of me?' asked Drudge.

'Will it have a name? What shall we call it?' asked Dent.

'Wait and see,' said Mrs Dippy firmly, as she sawed and screwed and fiddled and tinkered.

At last the car was ready. It was a very unusual kind of car.

'It doesn't look like a car,' said Drudge slowly.

'Will it go?' asked Dent. He looked worried.

'Of course it will,' said Mrs Dippy crossly. 'You're a perfectly good beach-buggy, aren't you Dally?'

'Beep!' said Dally.

'She talks!' cried the two robots with glee. 'Wow!'

'Time to pack,' said Mrs Dippy, looking proudly at Dally.

Dally was soon packed up with the picnic and beach things.

'Off we go now, Dally,' said Mrs Dippy at the wheel, and off they went. As they travelled, Drudge and Dent looked around them. There was so much to see.

'Look at that castle,' bleeped Drudge. Everyone looked at the castle.

'Look at that tree!' buzzed Dent. Everyone looked at the tree. But it was too late. BANG!

There were bits everywhere. The only one left in one piece was Mrs Dippy.

'Lucky I brought my tool kit,' she said seriously, picking a screw out of a sardine sandwich.

'Now let's get these machines put back together in a sensible sort of a way. There's still time for a good day out if I get on with it. I suppose to start with I'd better sort out which bits are which...'

They were soon all ready to set off
again.

'I'm tired,' said Dally. 'Can you
carry me?'

'Vroom, vroom,' said Drudge.
'Let's go!'

'Beep, beep,' said Dent.

'There's something not quite right here,' said Mrs Dippy. 'I think I'd better take another look at your insides.'

Mrs Dippy's machines were soon back together again. This time they were all making the right noises.

'Buzz wuzz,' barked Dent, jumping on to the sofa seat.

'Bleep, bleep,' crackled Drudge, climbing in slowly.

'Beep, beep,' tooted Dally, rocking on her wheels.

'That's more like it,' said Mrs Dippy, getting into the driver's seat once again.

'To the sea!' they all cried, as they drove off into the sunshine.

After a while Drudge said he could see something glittering far away.

'It's all sort of silvery-blue and shiny,' he bleeped.

'That's the sea,' said Mrs Dippy.
'It's where we're going.'

'What's it made of?' bleeped
Drudge.

'It's made of water, of course,' Mrs
Dippy explained.

'We don't have to wash up in it, do we?' bleeped Drudge, looking worried. 'Or do any laundry there?' he added, looking even more worried.

'Wait and see,' smiled Mrs Dippy.

'Here we are,' said Mrs Dippy, parking Dally neatly on the beach. 'This is the seaside. Isn't it nice?'

'I'm going to lie down and rest on the sand,' bleeped Drudge, settling down for a good snooze.

'And I'm going to do some doggy digging next to Drudge,' said Dent.

'And I'm going to invent a deckchair to sit in,' said Mrs Dippy. 'I brought the bits with me, specially for it.'

'Just a minute,' she said, before getting down to work, 'where's Drudge?'

Drudge was buried in sand. Only the top of his head was showing.

'Bad boy,' she said to Dent. 'Dig him up at once! He'll get sand in his workings and then anything could happen. Now, where's Dally? Oh dear.' The tide had come right in and Dally was surrounded by water.

'Look out!' bleeped Drudge. 'She'll get washed up!'

'Don't worry,' said Mrs Dippy. She got a TV channel flicker from her bag. She pressed a button and the umbrellas flipped over to make floats, so that Dally was like a boat.

'I was keeping that as a surprise for you. Aren't I clever? Now, who would like a trip around the bay in

Dally the floating car? All aboard!'

Mrs Dippy and her two robots climbed in and set off.

'What a lot of water,' bleeped Drudge nervously. 'It reminds me of the kitchen sink.'

'Buzz wuzz!' barked Dent. He had seen a catfish.

'What's that coming towards us?' bleeped Drudge. 'Is it a robot fish?'

'No!' said Mrs Dippy. 'It's a submarine and it's going to crash into us. But don't worry... I've got a special emergency button. Hold tight, everybody, here we go....'

What do you think will happen next?